One Night

a story from the desert

by **Cristina Kessler**

illustrated by **Ian Schoenherr**

Philomel Books   New York

*A special thanks to Muhamad,
Abdoulai, Aliou, and Joe—C.K.*

For Esther—I.S.

Author's Note

The Tuaregs' traditional lifestyle may soon become history. As
nomads, they have not fit well into the laws and ways of govern-
ment, made for sedentary cultures. The efforts to force them to
conform threaten the Tuaregs today.

   For this reason, it is very important to me to celebrate the
Tuareg spirit which connects them to light and space, freedom
and dignity. Let us hope that Muhamad's generation is not the
last to learn and practice a life where family and Mother Nature
are valued above all else.

Cristina Kessler

Al Hamdillilai, also *Al Hamdulillah* (al HUM-dil-lee-LIE, al HUM-dul-lee-LAH) Praise Allah
Erbiki (air-BEE-key) Hide-and-seek
At sunset the Tuareg people bow to the East toward Mecca, their holy city.

Text copyright © 1995 by Cristina Kessler. Illustrations copyright © 1995 by Ian Schoenherr.
All rights reserved. This book, or parts thereof, may not be reproduced in any form without permission
in writing from the publisher, Philomel Books, a division of The Putnam & Grosset Group, 200 Madison Avenue,
New York, NY 10016. Philomel Books, Reg. U.S. Pat. & Tm. Off. Published simultaneously in Canada.
Printed in Hong Kong by South China Printing Co. (1988) Ltd. Book design by Patrick Collins.
The text is set in Trump Mediaeval.

Library of Congress Cataloging-in-Publication Data   Kessler, Cristina. One night: a story from the desert /
Cristina Kessler; illustrated by Ian Schoenherr.   p.   cm.   Summary: When one of his goats gives birth, Muhamad
spends the night alone in the desert and thus becomes a man in the eyes of his family. [1. Tuaregs—Fiction.
2. Sahara—Fiction.]   I. Schoenherr, Ian. ill.   II. Title. PZ7.K4824A1   1995   [E]—dc20   94-6734 CIP AC
ISBN 0-399-22726-1   10 9 8 7 6 5 4 3 2 1   First Impression

I am Muhamad, son of Arahid, son of Zeinebu,
brother of two sisters and three brothers, all healthy.
I am the wealthiest of boys.
We are Tuaregs, some say the Blue People.
Our days begin with the first pale light in the east
and end around campfires that glow
golden in the desert nights.
Al Hamdillilai!

Mornings are good. But what I like are the nights
of Tam Tams, when the women play drums and sing our history.
My mother sings of the days when Tuareg men controlled the far
reaches of the desert, riding their courageous camels.
Her voice wanders high and low as she sings of Abouboukoum,
the camel from my father's youth. My father listens
and nods as she sings of its beauty and bravery.
"Remember," the women sing, "Tuaregs are the Princes
of the Earth. To be human is to be free. To be free is to be Tuareg."
Freedom in life is most important.
Al Hamdillilai!

A grandmother is a Tuareg boy's first teacher.
It is my grandmother who taught me
how to hear the viper as it burrows in the sand.
How to cure the sting of the scorpion.
"Leave no path, disturb no rock," my grandmother says
each day. "Make no changes on the earth, the desert
is fair to someone who knows how to live with it."

And she says each day, "You are the best in all.
The strongest, the most handsome, a true camel man."
I am the wealthiest of boys.
Al Hamdillilai!

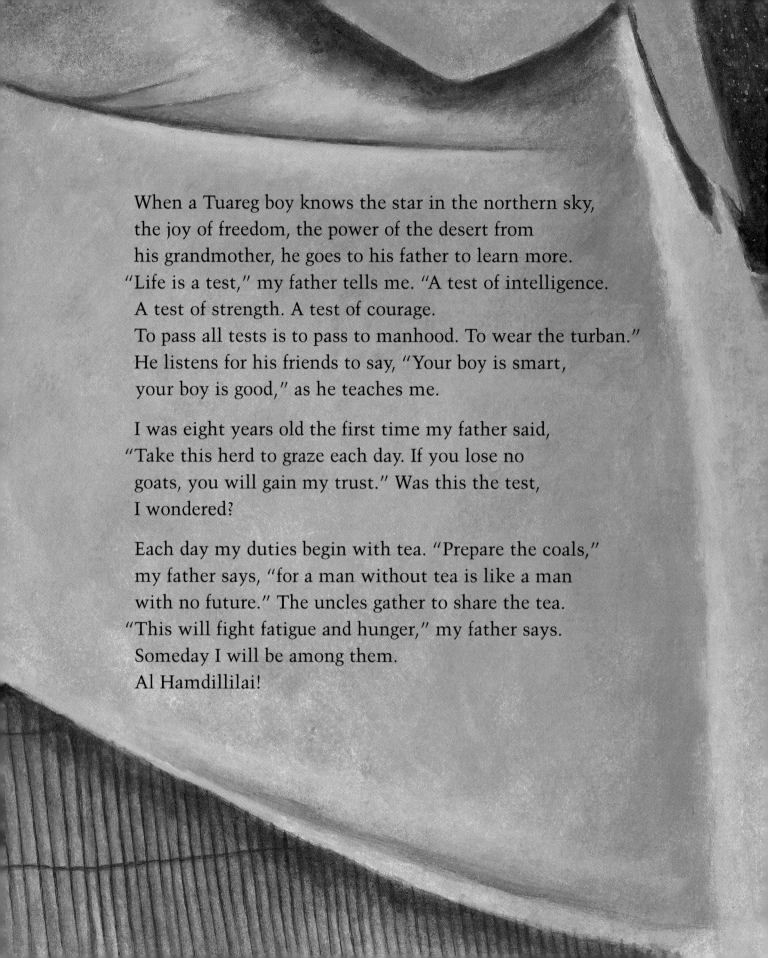

When a Tuareg boy knows the star in the northern sky,
the joy of freedom, the power of the desert from
his grandmother, he goes to his father to learn more.
"Life is a test," my father tells me. "A test of intelligence.
A test of strength. A test of courage.
To pass all tests is to pass to manhood. To wear the turban."
He listens for his friends to say, "Your boy is smart,
your boy is good," as he teaches me.

I was eight years old the first time my father said,
"Take this herd to graze each day. If you lose no
goats, you will gain my trust." Was this the test,
I wondered?

Each day my duties begin with tea. "Prepare the coals,"
my father says, "for a man without tea is like a man
with no future." The uncles gather to share the tea.
"This will fight fatigue and hunger," my father says.
Someday I will be among them.
Al Hamdillilai!

But now each morning I take the herd to graze.
"Take a friend," my father always says.
"Go with your brother," my mother always advises.
But always I leave in the early dawn light,
alone with my goats.

The open sky is my roof. The stars, my connection
to the night. I have no secrets from the sky
as I go, and no one can take the sky from me.

I taste the wind on my tongue
and feel the sun touch my heart
as finally I sit with my goats while they graze.
Yes, I am the wealthiest of boys.

The desert is my floor. The rocks, my pasture
where water gathers and little plants grow.
There my goats can graze among the rocks.
"Be at one with your surroundings and you will
be at peace," my grandmother always says.
Al Hamdillilai!

My ears hear all that is happening.
The wings of passing birds and desert mice
quickly running across the sand.
The soft sound of goats pulling leaves from the trees.
The busy sound of termites working in their hills.
"The most powerful secrets are with nature,
not with man," my grandmother always says.

"Respect nature and be powerful."
I hear the voice of my grandmother and the wind
across the sand. Never do I lose a goat. I return
with all my herd. I hear the *thunk-thunk* of my aunt
pounding millet and know my herd and I are home.

It is during the days of Ramadan;
the sun slides toward the horizon. I click my tongue
to gather the goats and start our long walk home.

Allah makes the markers to find my way.
Some are red termite hills
higher than my uncle's turban.
Others are acacia trees
with branches as thin as spider's web.

It is just before sunset when I notice
one fat mother goat falling behind.
"What is it, Mother?" I ask the goat.
She looks at me with soft brown eyes,
then lies down in the sand. I touch her belly.
"We will pass the night here," I announce to the herd,
"for I must deliver safely all goats to my father,
and I know soon we shall be one more."

I realize this will be my first night alone in the desert.
I strain to hear *thunk-thunk, thunk-thunk,*
the sound of my aunt pounding millet.
I hear only my own pounding heart.
I gather the scrub brush loose on the ground
to build a goat pen for the night.
The goats bleat, their udders too full.

When night begins to overtake the day,
the sky turns orange.
"Acknowledge the sunset each day,"
my grandmother always says. I bow to the East,
thanking Allah for the moment
of mercy when the sun leaves the sky.
Thanking Allah for another day.
Al Hamdillilai!

As the moon rises to greet me, I milk the goats.
My dinner. In my mind's eye I see my sister
arrange the sleeping mats.
I see my cousins play *erbiki*, my favorite game.

The sounds of the night replace the sounds of the day.
I sit and listen for the lion that no longer
walks the land.

At camp I know the women prepare
the evening meal. My father drinks tea with
the uncles and his friends in the day's moment
of true relaxation. His eyes are surer than mine.
"It is time for the brown and white goat to drop
her baby," my father will tell his friends.
"Tonight Muhamad may not come home." Lifting his tea,
he will say, "I know my son will do well."

In the stillness of the darkening night I hear
the short breaths of the she-goat. "Relax, Mother,
we will stay as long as you need," I whisper in her ear,
and I touch her full belly. My grandmother's words,
"Let nature lead," echo through my mind.

The she-goat and I are both new to the experience
of giving life. It is her first kid and also mine.
Yes, I am the wealthiest of boys.

Hours pass by.
My thoughts are loud in a night
filled only with the music of crickets.

A sudden bleat from the mother goat
shocks the night. A soft thump
follows as the new baby goat drops
to the earth. I run to the mother
and tell her, "It is beautiful."
Al Hamdillilai!

Lying in the dark, I smile. One day
my sister shall sing of this night
at Cure Salee. In my mind's eye I see
all the Tuaregs gather from across the desert
to race and trade their finest camels and meet
with family and friends. To celebrate the survival
of another year. To tell tales of days past.
This night, my first a true nomad, will be sung
again and again at the Cure Salees to come.
My eyes begin to close. I thank Allah again
for another day in paradise.
Al Hamdillilai!

Life is a test, and I have succeeded.
It is the she-goat's first kid, and
the beginning of my own herd. I sleep.

In the morning, I see the star
in the northern sky that acts as my compass.

"Let's go home," I tell my herd. Gently,
I take the kid in my arms and click to
my goats to begin the walk home.

Before I see camp I hear the *thunk-thunk*
of mortar and pestle. The sweet smell of fresh
tea floats on the air. The distant voices of herders
calling their herds fills my ears.

My sister Jadijitu runs to me and shouts
a greeting. Zeinebu, my mother, wraps me in
her black gown to welcome me home.
My uncle Abdoulai takes the new goat from my arms.
"Your son, the man, has returned," he tells my father.

My father pats the ground beside him. I sit.
He hands me a glass of tea.
"The herd looks well," my father says.
"The family is well," my mother adds.
My father looks at my mother. "It is time
to buy a turban for Muhamad, a fine blue one."
I smile inside.
I know once again I am the wealthiest of boys.
Al Hamdillilai!

DATE			